God the Father
and the
Best Day Ever

Gracie Jagla

Illustrated by
Jacob Popcak

Huntington, Indiana

25 24 23 22 21 20   1 2 3 4 5 6 7 8 9

Our Sunday Visitor Publishing Division
Our Sunday Visitor, Inc.
200 Noll Plaza
Huntington, IN 46750
www.osv.com
1-800-348-2440

ISBN: 978-1-68192-440-3 (Inventory No. T2325)
1. JUVENILE FICTION—Religious—Christian—Holidays & Celebrations. 2. JUVENILE FICTION—Holidays & Celebrations—Easter & Lent. 3. RELIGION—Christianity—Catholic.

LCCN: 2019951493

Cover and interior design: Tyler Ottinger
Cover art: Jacob Popcak
Interior art: Jacob Popcak

PRINTED IN THE UNITED STATES OF AMERICA

To my mom, whose childlike joy in the Faith inspires me always, and to my dad, my very first example of the Father's love.

You've heard Easter's story,
You know how it goes:
Christ died for our sins
And on Easter, he rose.

But there's more to the story
That you might not know.
What happened above when God
Triumphed below?

To understand that,
We must go to the start,
When God formed creation,
His grand work of art.

At time's first beginning,
God made us a home,
Where we could be with him
And happily roam.

But when we first sinned,
Heaven's strong gates grew shut.
Nobody could open them,
No matter what.

For many long years,
People just had to wait.
But God had a plan
To reopen the gate.

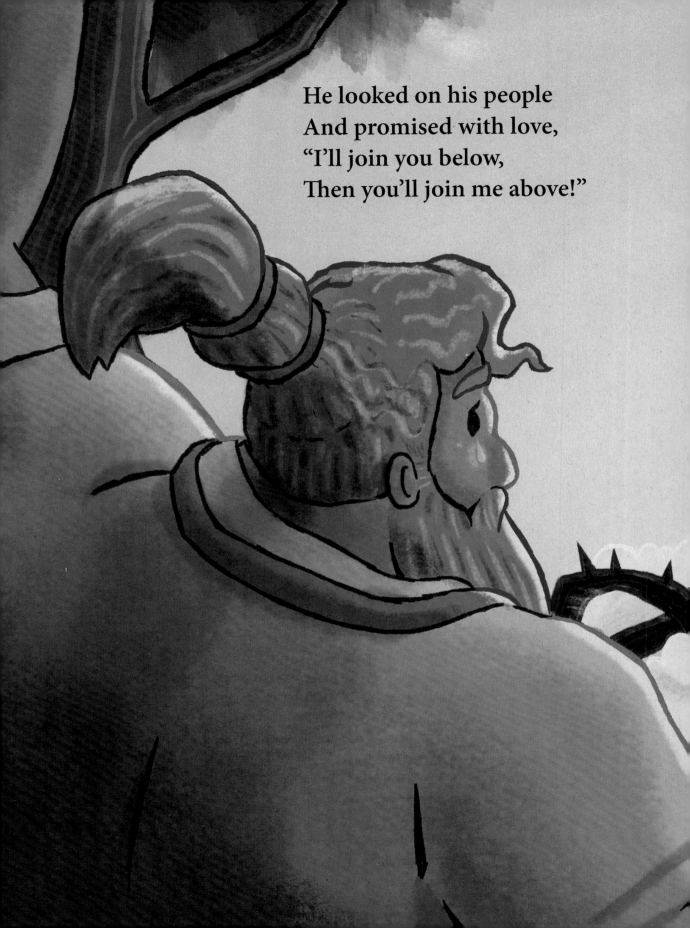

He looked on his people
And promised with love,
"I'll join you below,
Then you'll join me above!"

He sent his Son down
The first cold Christmas day.
Later, his death washed
Our sins all away.

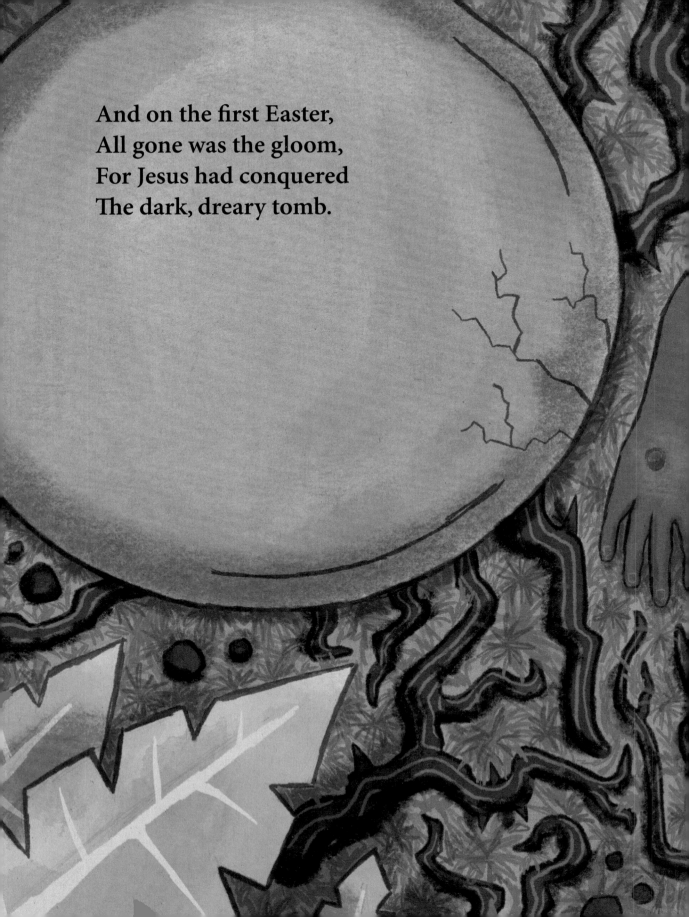

And on the first Easter,
All gone was the gloom,
For Jesus had conquered
The dark, dreary tomb.

Remember for so long
The gates that were closed?
Well, all of that changed
Just the second Christ rose!

He opened those overgrown
Gates with a thrust.
His heart was so joyful,
He thought it might bust.

Now that the gates had been
Opened so wide,
People could come and
Fill up the inside!

And flood in they did,
Saints from all through the years,
With smiling and cheering
And even some tears.

Some sang, others danced,
And they twirled all about,
Between hugging and laughing
And heavenly shouts.

A place once deserted
Was now filled with noise,
With the sound of each saintly
And angelic voice.

Then God bent down low
And with tender embrace,
Kissed every head and each
Smiling face.

These children he loved
And had missed for so long
Were now his forever!
To him, they belonged.

This party in Heaven
Continues today;
The joy of God's love
Will not fade away.

And you can go too,
If you share in his love,
Join with the saints
Up in Heaven above.

Since Jesus rose up
And reopened the gates,
The promise of paradise
For us awaits.

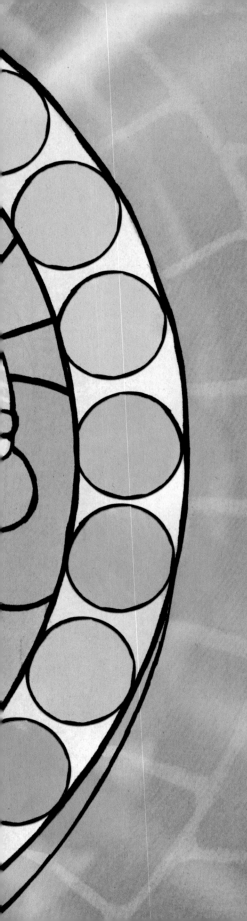

That's why we love Easter,
Since, thanks to this day,
We can see God in Heaven,
Forever to stay!